BEES AND HONEY

A SWAMP MONSTER LOVE STORY

VICTORIA WEYLAND

To All who Prefer Monsters

ONE

"Get you some of that ancient vampire tushy," I murmured, turning the page of my tattered book.

Water slowly lapped against the mooring piles. *Swamp Ass*, my aluminum flat-bottomed boat, bumped against the dock, sending up a dull *thunk* with each collision. The noise was accompanied by the occasional cry of a heron or the plunk of a turtle sliding into the water from a floating log. A breeze cut through the oppressive heat of the late afternoon and tugged at the brown curls that had escaped my ponytail.

A high-pitched whine flew past my ear and landed on the tanned stretch of thigh spreading from my cutoff shorts.

"Nope. I only like my bloodsuckers fictional." The paperback hit my leg with a loud *thwack*. When I lifted it away, all that was left was a smear of bug bits and blood. "Ew."

After wiping off the remains, I leaned back in my lawn chair and propped my foot on the top of one pylon. The heroine was just about to get that undead dick when a shadow fell across the page.

I didn't bother to look up. "Better have brought me a beer."

"Don't I always, girlie?"

A sweating bottle of PBR came into view. Condensation dripped onto the page as I took it. After taking a long swig, I tilted my head up and grinned at Bubs as he eased his large frame into the lawn chair next to mine and set the rest of a six-pack by his feet.

"Couldn't spring for an Abita Amber?"

Bubs let out one of his full-body laughs, his shoulders shaking. A PBR bottle rested on his denim overall covered beer keg of a belly. Since it was summer, he wasn't wearing a shirt and, as usual, his white skin was ruddy with the sun. A salt-and-pepper beard hung from his chin, like Spanish moss clinging to a limb.

One bushy white eyebrow rose, even as his dark eyes danced with mirth. "When ya're buying the beers, Heather, you can shell out for the good stuff."

"Fair enough." I tipped my head in acknowledgment before leaning over and letting a bit of beer fall into the murky waters below. "To Honey."

Shaking his head at my ritual, Bubs said, "The way Ol' Benny tells it, you should leave the Honey Island Swamp Monster gifts of secondhand clothes, not beer."

"Did the old geezer get drunk and lose his shorts in the bayou again?"

"Yep."

"Typical Benny," I said with a shake of my head. "It's a wonder the man hasn't been eaten by an alligator or split that hard head of his on a cypress knee."

Using the hem of my tank top, I brushed the water

droplets from the page. Bub's shadow blocked the light again.

"…her hands gently squeezed his velvety balls, causing his massive cock to jump in response," Bubs read aloud. The shadow disappeared. "Let me borrow that when ya're done."

"Ha. No way. Cliff will skin my ass. The last time I leant you a vamp book, you went all honey badger on him. His neck looked like an amorous nutria had mauled him."

"The man likes to grumble, but he can't get enough of my love nibbles," Bubs replied, punctuating his words with a jab of his beer bottle.

I grinned and shook my head. We sat in companionable silence, drinking our beer. The distant drone of an outboard motor cut through the sounds of the swamp: the buzz of insects, the lap of water, and the calls of birds.

"Evening, Zeke," I called as the middle-aged Black man slowed down to pull up along the edge of the dock. His short afro was going thin at the crown of his head, but he still had the well-muscled torso of someone who worked long hours of hard labor.

"Heather. Bubs. How's things?"

"Hotter than Satan's house cat and it's not even July. Beer?" Bubs grabbed a beer and held it out.

"Much obliged." With practiced skill, Zeke heaved himself up on the dock without tipping his boat and retrieved the beer. He settled back and opened the bottle with a twist of his hand.

"How's work?" I asked, creasing a corner of the page and closing my book.

"Never-ending as always." Zeke had a small auto body shop and also fixed the occasional outboard motor. He reached down and pulled a couple of catfish on a line from the water-filled cooler in the bottom of his boat. "Delilah said y'all worked out a trade."

"We sure did." I grabbed the mason jar of honey from where it sat on a post, stood up, and traded him for the fish.

Zeke nodded in thanks as he wrapped the jar in an old T-shirt and tucked it into the bottom of the boat. "Delilah's making her blueberry-honey upside-down cake for the church bake-off and swears that only your honey will do."

Fun Bee Fact: Bees must collect nectar from about two million flowers to make a pound of honey.

"Tell her to put a couple of slices aside for Cliff and me," Bubs said as I knelt down on the sun-warmed boards and tied the fish to the line that looped around the last pillar of the dock.

Everyone in the swamp knew Cliff and Bubs were married, maybe not in the eyes of the State, but definitely in the eyes of each other. Folks around that part of the swamp all had our own reasons for being there, and folks' business was their own. But it was still Southern Louisiana. While they probably wouldn't be turned away at the church bake sale, they wouldn't exactly be welcome either. Then again, neither would I. One of the paperback romances I'd gotten from the used bookstore in Slidell taught me the term *pansexual,* and it seemed the closest I'd found to describing my sexuality. Bubs loved to remind me, "Us swamp gays have to stick together."

"I'll make sure she stops by the house." Zeke took a

long drink of his beer. He kept his eyes out on the swamp as he said, "You heard about the Mileys?"

My heart sank into my stomach. "Don't tell me they sold out to that bloodsucker who's been hounding us for the last few months."

Zeke's mouth tightened into a disapproving line as he nodded.

"Shiiiiiiit" was Bubs's reply. Bubs could turn that particular word from one syllable to at least four.

The Mileys lived on the land next to mine, on the opposite side from Cliff and Bubs. I turned to look toward their house, but of course I couldn't see it from here. The river curved right after my dock, and between that and the swath of trees separating our properties, I sometimes forgot the family was even there.

"The money was just too good," Zeke lamented.

Hard to argue with that when they had three kids. Not when their little two-room house was one strong breeze away from tumbling into the bayou. Folks got to do what's best for themselves, but damn if it didn't leave a bitter taste in my mouth.

"You folks are the last ones left."

Bubs and I looked at each other. He had that belligerent, stubborn look he sometimes got. The one that drove Cliff batty because it usually meant he'd have to bail Bubs out of trouble, or worse, out of jail.

I grinned widely at him and held out my beer. The clink of his nearly empty bottle colliding with mine was a comforting sound, one this dock had heard often in the ten years I'd been living on the edge of the Honey Island Swamp. No corporate fat cat with deep pockets was going to pry us from our homes. Not when I knew what they'd planned to do with the land. Despite the day's heat, a little shudder ran down my spine.

"Well, I'd better be gettin' back to Delilah. She'll be itching to get that cake started." Zeke finished his beer and set the empty bottle on the edge of the dock. After exchanging farewell nods all around, Zeke started up his outboard with a swift pull. Deftly, he maneuvered the boat around and headed off into the swamp.

Once his motor had faded into the distance, the familiar sounds of the swamp returned, but the peace of my afternoon was shattered. I felt restless and antsy, like someone had stirred up one of my hives and poured bees under my skin.

"Hey, girlie," Bubs cut through my worrying. "Why don't I take those fish and do a proper fish fry tonight? Cliff's got a pot of collards on the stove. They'd go mighty fine together."

A grateful grin pulled at the corners of my mouth. "When Delilah called, I'd hoped you'd offer. You know I'm worthless when it comes to fish."

With a grunt, Bubs heaved himself out of his chair. He collected the empty bottles and set them back in the six-pack, along with the three unopened ones. "You want to come up to the house and keep me company while I cook? Might even learn something."

"I would, but I need to check on the hives before it gets dark."

One meaty hand gave my shoulder a quick squeeze, before Bubs gathered up the catfish and lumbered down the dock toward shore.

"Bubs."

He paused and looked back at me.

"Thank you."

His weathered red face sprouted more wrinkles as he grinned. "No problem, girlie. Us swamp gays got to stick together."

Fun Bee Fact: Honey Island Swamp, a twenty-mile nature reserve, is named for its honey bees.

Tucking my book into my back pocket, I hiked up the gentle slope of the hill that led from the dock to the house. My cabin sat tucked up against the trees to the right, close to Bubs and Cliff's property line. When I'd moved into the two-bedroom, one-bath home with its tiny kitchen and sagging porch, I'd been twenty-eight years old and angry. Angry at the world, my asshole ex with his wandering eye, and society at large. I'd known fuck all about bees, but I sure as shit was gonna learn.

Cliff and Bubs had stopped by and helped unload the back of my truck, which contained all my worldly possessions at that point. Even in my haze of rage, I'd been so relieved to find out I was living next to like-minded folk. I hadn't meant the relationship hiatus to be permanent, but between learning the ropes to keep the bee colonies happy and healthy and setting up my honey business, I hadn't had a lot of time for dating. I was mostly content with my romance novels. Oh, and my trusty vibrator.

I took the trail to where my thirty hives lived. When I'd first bought the property, there had only been ten hives—all a mess. Armed with books from the library and a lot of help from Cliff and Bubs, I'd rebuilt the leaning, rotted hives and then later expanded bit by bit to my current apiary. Even though I only had an acre cleared, I'd done what I could to plant wildflowers and other pollinator-enticing plants like prairie clover, asters, wild hyacinth, bluebonnets, and bee balm. Still, a lot of the nectar and pollen my bees gathered came from the swamp just across the way. It was filled with milkweed and waterlilies, perfect for my buzzing buddies.

Fun Bee Fact: Bees can fly between four and six miles a day foraging for nectar and pollen.

At the edge of the clearing was my equipment shed, lovingly referred to as the Honey Hut. A scarred workbench held the various tools I used for taking care of the hives. I grabbed my smoker. It looked a little like the oil can Dorothy used to revive the Tin Man, but with a shorter nozzle. Flipping over the lid, I stuffed some pine needles and bits of cardboard into the fuel reservoir. After grabbing the lighter from its hook on the wall, I lit another bit of cardboard and carefully tucked in with the rest. Soon I had a good smolder going and I screwed on the lid. Since the bellows controlled the oxygen, the fire in a smoker could last for several hours. I donned my work gloves and my cowboy hat, pulling the fine mesh veil down around my face.

Fun Bee Fact: Apparently, there's no actual word for the protective headgear used for beekeeping. It's just called a hat and a veil. Seems like a missed opportunity.

Summer was the busy season for my bee babies. They scrambled like mad to store up reserves for the winter, taking advantage of all the plants in bloom, getting their stamen on. That meant it was prime honey season for me. The clearing was alive with the sound of buzzing wings and zig-zagging black-and-yellow bodies.

Pumping the bellows on the smoker, I approached the

Earnhardt hive with the faded red No. 3 paint job Bubs had done in a fit of NASCAR nostalgia and moonshine. It was also the first hive I'd successfully harvested when I started the farm. It held a special place in my heart.

Fun Bee Fact: A single colony can be home to up to 50,000 bees.

"Good afternoon, darlins," I crooned in a low, soothing voice. The smoke wreathed the hive as I approached it from behind. The bees darting in and out of the wooden structure slowed their mad flight, their movements becoming slow and lazy. There's some debate in the bee world (you might call it a *bee*-bate) about how the smoke works. Some think it inhibits the bees' panic receptors, while others think it reminds the bees of a forest fire and they gorge on honey in preparation for fleeing the hive. I don't really care one way or the other so long as it calms them down and allows me to check on the combs without distressing them. Or getting stung.

Considering how many times I've been stung over the years, I was kind of used to it by that point. But it was still annoying and it killed the poor bee.

After hooking the smoker to the rusty ring on the side of the hive, I took off the top. Bees crawled over the ten frames hanging in the top box of the hive. A few more pumps of the smoker sent a gray cloud swirling through the frames.

"Now, let's see what's what, hmm?" I pulled one frame out. It was almost covered in honeycomb, capped with wax, and filled with golden honey. This particular frame had no brood cells and I couldn't see the queen with her swarm of attendant bees.

I slid the frame back and checked another one. "A day. Two more at the most. Then we'll get to harvesting that sweet, sweet gold."

"Do you always talk to your bees?"

Only ten years of working with bees kept me from screaming and dropping the frame. Not only would that have destroyed the frame, but my bees would definitely have taken it as a sign of aggression and attacked. Then they would have died and my night would have been ruined and it would have all been that bloodsucking asshole's fault.

"McMaster." I ground his name out through clenched teeth as I carefully set the frame back into its place and secured the lid.

"Heather. I've told you before: please, call me Clayton."

I turned around, instinctively placing myself between him and the hive, and crossed my arms over my chest. "What do you want, McMaster?"

McMaster's good-boy grin faltered for a second before plastering itself back in place. A white man in his early thirties, he was tall with the shoulders of a high-school football star that strained his tight blue polo shirt. Two interlocking *M*s were embroidered in gold thread on the shirt.

"I was hoping you'd reconsidered my generous offer."

I cocked my head to the side. "What part of 'take your offer and shove it' made you think I'd be reconsidering?"

He tilted his head toward me, his hands coming up in a placating motion. If I didn't think it would do more damage to my smoker, I'd have been real tempted to smack him upside his thick skull with it.

"Now, there's no need to be uncivil. We're just having a friendly discussion. I'm sure by now you've heard that your neighbors took me up on my generous offer. You're the last piece of the puzzle."

A shitty puzzle.

McMaster put his hands in the pockets of his dark wash jeans and I couldn't help but notice his pristine alligator cowboy boots. These didn't look like they'd come from the local Walmart. They had to cost a pretty penny, and who the hell wears expensive cowboy boots in the swamp?

"I've run the numbers and we're willing to go ten percent above the last offer." He gave me a big, generous smile. "What do ya say?"

It was a lot of money. There was no denying that, but even if I took it, where would I go? Where would my bees go? This was our home. "That is indeed a fine offer."

McMaster's grin stretched into what could only be called "shit-eating".

"But." I picked up my smoker. "I have to decline."

His face clouded over, darker than a summer's thunderstorm. "Wait a minute, now—"

"Nothin' to wait for," I cut him off with a shake of my head. "Now get the hell off my property before I send my bees after you."

He looked around in alarm at the cloud of black, buzzing bodies over the field before narrowing his eyes at me.

I raised one shoulder in a shrug. It was worth a shot.

"You sure there's no way we can come to some sort of agreement? There must be some way I can sweeten this deal for you. Everyone has a price."

"I'm not selling, no matter how 'sweet' the offer. Now buzz off."

The congenial mask was gone. A finger came up to point at me. If he'd been closer, he would have loomed over me. Probably used to using his size to intimidate folks.

"Look here, you—! *SON OF A BITCH!*" He swung his hand around while taking several steps backward.

Huh. Maybe attack bees were a thing, after all. I felt bad for the bee, but her sacrifice was appreciated.

McMaster let out another string of curses before clutching his hand to his chest and glaring at me as if I'd personally stung him. "This project is going forward with or without your infested bit of swamp. By the time I'm finished, you'll be begging me to take your worthless land off your hands. Just you see."

Well, I was going to suggest he put a bit of honey on the sting—it is antibacterial after all—but with an attitude like that, his ass could suffer. "Best get off my property. Now that one attacked, the hives know a threat is about. They'll swarm if you're not careful."

With one last glare in my direction, he scurried away in his fancy cowboy boots. Anger simmered in my chest, but I pushed it aside with a sigh and placed a hand on the top of the hive.

"Don't worry about that big ol' meanie. He's a lot of bluster and no balls. I won't let anything happen to you, my sweets. We just got to *bee* positive."

TWO

Despite my best efforts, I couldn't seem to follow my own advice.

"You're brooding awful hard," Cliff said, pushing a fresh bottle of beer into my hands as he eased himself into his favorite chair at their kitchen table.

A few years older than his partner, Cliff was rail thin to Bubs's generous belly. His grey hair was kept in a short afro and his dark-brown skin was wrinkled from the sun and time.

I forced a smile onto my face as I dragged a finger through condensation on my beer bottle. Not even Bubs's excellent fried fish or Cliff's mouthwatering collard greens had been enough to shake the sense of foreboding that had settled into my bones after the encounter with McMaster.

"Don't pay that puffed up weasel no mind!" came Bubs's shout over the sound of running water and the clink of dishes.

"Easier said than done," I replied before taking a deep drink of my beer. My thoughts kept coming back to

McMaster's threats like bees to a tasty patch of wildflowers. "I just have this feeling he's not gonna give up."

"That's because no one told that overprivileged white boy no in his life. But you don't have to face him alone." Cliff reached over and patted my arm. "As my Bubs always says…"

The smile was real as I recited with Cliff, "Us swamp gays got to stick together."

"Damn straight!" Bubs shouted.

After giving my arm one more squeeze, Cliff let go and speared me with a look I knew all too well.

"Nah-ah. You are not hooking me up on another terrible date."

Cliff held up his hands in a defensive motion. "You ain't even heard who it is."

"I don't need to know who it is. Not interested."

He clucked his tongue at me while shaking his head slowly. "Just because you had a bad relationship—" My snort had him amending his statement. "—a couple of bad relationships—doesn't mean you need to spend the rest of your life on your lonesome. Young thing like you shouldn't spend all your time with two old farts."

"I happen to like you two old farts better than pretty much everyone else. And I also spend time with Patty and Miguel."

"While us old farts love you too, I wish you'd give Keely a chance. She's a sweet pea."

"I'm sure she is, but I'm still not interested in dating."

Before Cliff could argue, Bubs's hand came down on his shoulder. "Leave the girlie alone, Cliff."

"But Keely's a fine girl."

Bubs lowered himself into a chair and opened up a fresh beer. "No doubt about that, but Keely's a city girl. Our Heather needs someone who has swamp water running through their veins and dreams of never leaving the bayou. The right person's out there for her, but it does no good to push her."

"Thank you!" I leaned my bottle over for Bubs to clink with his.

Bubs's other hand reached out to link with Cliff's. "'Sides, our girl's as stubborn as a mule and twice as hardheaded."

"Hey!"

Cliff's thin shoulders shook with laughter as I looked for something to chuck at Bubs's head.

That night, sleep was an elusive beast. The Mileys selling out and McMaster's dogged persistence made me feel like my sanctuary had been invaded after so many years of safety. McMaster's threats had gotten under my skin and wouldn't let me be. So I did the next best thing: tried to drown my worried thoughts in bourbon.

Fun Bee Fact: Bees can, in fact, get drunk. Though, usually it's off fermented fruit and not Wild Turkey.

When most of the bottle was gone but my worries remained, I grabbed the bottle and a bag of marshmallows and headed down to the dock.

As the boards rolled under my feet, I worked hard not to end up in the water and lose my shorts like Benny had. It was harder than it should have been, but I was already over halfway and there was no turning back. I let out a little woof of breath as I flopped onto the end of the dock and dangled my legs over the edge. Thankfully, I was too short for my toes to hit the water and become tasty little niblets for any passing fish or snake.

The swamp at night had a surreal beauty to it— almost alien in the glint of the moon on the water and the croak of the frogs calling to each other. Lightning bugs flitted between the trees, trailing bright pinpricks of light. It was still hotter than sin, but a cool breeze blew, making it bearable. I took in a deep breath and let out a long sigh.

"What am I going to do?" I said in a low voice. "There's not enough money in the world for me to leave the swamp or my bees… but I don't think Asshole is gonna give up. I'm worried about what he'll try next."

The only answer was the chirp of crickets and a faraway splash of some swamp creature plopping into the water.

Keeping one hand firmly wrapped around a post, I leaned out and dumped the last of my bourbon into the water. "No chance you'd send your Swamp Monster to eat him, huh?"

"Can't help but think that someone named 'Asshole' wouldn't taste real good."

A startled squeak escaped me as I yanked my feet up and scooted back from the edge of the dock. My heart thundered in my chest and my eyes scanned the dark water, the still reeds on the bank, and the far shore. All empty. A part of me worried McMaster had come to kill me off in the night, but I didn't recognize that rough, deep Southern accent.

"Wh-who's there?"

The sound of water moving came from under the end of the dock. "You know who I am, especially considerin' you just spilled a tribute in my name."

Shock stilled my movements as the word "Honey" slipped from my lips.

A low chuckle burned through my fear and sent a flare of heat into my belly. Holy moly, what the heck was wrong with me? I should have been running for the hills or to Bubs and Cliff for safety, not finding disembodied voices sexy. Especially not a voice belonging to…

Two hands gripped the edge of the dock. Black claws at least two inches long dug into the soft wood. Water streamed off scaly, dark green skin, almost black in the moonlight, as the creature hoisted itself out of the water and stood upright on muscular hind legs.

Granted, my angle wasn't great, but Honey had to be at least six and a half feet tall. A pair of ragged jean shorts clung to slim hips. A broad chest and powerful shoulders supported a thick neck. My eyes climbed up further, my brain refusing to fully comprehend what stood in front of me. Thin lips pulled back to reveal sharp rows of teeth. There were two vertical slits where a nose should have been. The eyes that regarded me with keen, intelligent interest glowed gold in the moonlight.

I raised the half-empty bag still clutched in my hand. "Marshmallow?"

One heavily ridged brow raised. "Like what the tour boats throw to entice wild pigs and my brethren?"

Holy shit. They threw marshmallows from the tour boats to the gators so tourists could take pictures. My brain was so stuck on how yummy this creature was, it had completely forgotten that point. But I wasn't about to admit that fact, so I scrambled for another explanation.

"Yeah, but they're my favorite drunk food." I reached into the bag and pulled one of them out. I gave it a couple of test squishes as I rambled on. "They're sweet and chewy and I like how they squish. These are way better than the ones they use on the tours. Those are sugar-free. Better for the animals' tummies… Sure you don't want one?"

At that point, I'd nervously squished the marshmallow all to gummy hell and I desperately popped it into my mouth, leaving sticky residue all over my fingers and lips. The creature was definitely smirking at me now.

Maybe there'd be a freak wave and I'd be washed away from this mortifying situation. I was pretty sure drowning in swamp water would be a much better alternative.

The creature regarded me for a moment before it said, "All right."

"All right?" I repeated, but because my mouth was full of gooey marshmallow, it came more like "Awigth?"

Moving with a sensuous grace, Honey sank down near me. Only then did I notice the long, scaly tail that curled around Honey's side. It looked a lot like an alligator's tail, complete with a spiny ridge down the middle, but with more flexibility. The creature reached out a hand. Slowly and gently, Honey wrapped long, clawed fingers around my wrist. Jesus, Mary, and Joseph, Honey's hand was so large it made my beefy wrist seem small and dainty by comparison. Honey's skin was smooth and surprisingly soft, despite the scales. I couldn't help but wonder what that hand would feel like on other parts of my body.

Pull your drunk self together, woman!

Honey pulled my hand toward their mouth and its rows of sharp, pointy teeth. A distant part of my brain started sounding alarm bells. Maybe it was the massive amount of alcohol I'd consumed or the fact that this was Honey, a creature known for taking care of the swamp, but I wasn't interested in snatching my hand away or screaming for help. Instead, I held my breath, my whole being focused on the warm pressure of their hand on my wrist and the mischievous glint in their golden eyes.

"May I?" Honey asked, their voice a low rumble.

"Oh! Um. Sure."

Thin lips parted and a long tongue snaked out to wrap around my marshmallow-covered fingers. A shudder raced down my spine and liquid heat pooled between my thighs. There was a slightly rough texture to their tongue, like a cat's, and soon they'd licked every speck of gooey sugar from my fingertips.

"Delicious." Gently, Honey released my wrist and gave me a toothy smile that made me think they weren't talking about the marshmallow. But maybe that was just wishful thinking. "Thank you, Heather."

If I'd thought forming complete sentences was hard before…. Hang on a minute. "You know my name?"

Honey tilted their head to the side, their smile going even wider. "I know all the folks of the swamp. At least by sight, but old timers by name as well."

"Do you mind me calling you Honey? Or would you prefer something else? What about pronouns?"

"Male pronouns are fine. My name was lost long before men with rifles raided the swamps to strip them of their treasures." His smile slipped from his face and he gazed off over the water. "Honey is fine."

There was such a sadness to him, a weight of time and loss, and I found myself reaching out to pat his forearm. His very muscular forearm. When in the world had I developed a forearm fetish?

His hand covered mine, mindful of his claws. He gave me a small smile. "Enough lookin' back. Tell me about Asshole."

Oh right, I hadn't summoned Honey to ogle him. There was a threat to the swamp, or at least my little part of it.

Settling against a pillar, I explained about my bee farm

and McMaster's bid to get me to sell him my property. During my tale, I periodically pulled marshmallows out of the bag and handed half to Honey.

"… worst part is, he wants the land to build a country club and a golf course. It's something straight out of the Goonies!" I slumped against the post and held out the last marshmallow to Honey.

"Goonies?" he asked as he waved a hand at me.

"It's a classic. Bunch of kids go on an adventure to save their homes and there's booby traps and pirates," I mumbled around my mouthful of sugar. I was kind of wishing I hadn't drunk all my bourbon before coming down to the dock, or at least that I'd thought to grab my water bottle. "But you probably haven't seen a lot of movies…"

The head tilt was back, along with a grin. "No. Sometimes the Swamp Tour place plays movies on the wall in the evenings, but those're the only ones I've seen."

I'd been to many of Patty and Miguel's movie nights. It was strange to think that Honey had been there, watching from the shadows of the swamp. "Maybe we could do a movie night sometime?"

"I'd like that. But going back to your Asshole problem."

The phrase made me cringe. "Maybe we can just call him McMaster instead of Asshole. And I'm not sure what to do about him. Other than building ugly mansions for rich people, he's technically not doing anything wrong."

"Do you think he'll be good for the swamp?"

That was the question, wasn't it? "No. I don't think so. I've got this sick, foreboding feeling in my gut. You know how the swamp gets before a hurricane?"

Honey nodded slowly. "There's a tension in the air. Everything goes quiet. Like it's waiting."

"Exactly. Like it knows there's bad things on the horizon. That's how I feel about McMaster."

Honey nodded slowly. "I've been watching the changes happening. Machinery belching noise and smoke. Ancient trees felled to make way for sterile homes erected with no connection with the land."

Despite the seriousness of the subject, I had to stifle a yawn. It was getting late, or early, depending on how you looked at it, and the bourbon and massive amounts of sugar were making my brain and body fuzzy.

Honey sat up straighter, with his head cocked to one side. "Boat's a-coming."

"I don't hear anything."

One claw pointed down the waterway. The sound of a motor broke the pre-dawn stillness and cut through my drunken haze.

"Oh. You're right. Maybe you should…" I turned to find the dock empty. "…hide."

A small fishing boat came around the bend. Its passengers were coming in from night fishing or going out for some early morning fishing. The pair were decked out in camo and gave me a wave as they passed. I shook off my surprise enough to return their greeting and got to my feet. The sound of the boat faded and once again, the swamp was still and quiet.

Leaning over the end of the dock, I searched the dark water for any sign of golden eyes. Nothing. Had I made up talking to the legendary Honey Island Swamp Monster? Had it been a hallucination fueled by booze and fear of the future?

The swamp kept her secrets and the dawn was fast approaching. I needed to get to bed. After gathering up the empty marshmallow bag and bourbon bottle, I dragged myself up to the house and flopped onto the bed, not even bothering to take off my clothes. Despite my exhaustion, my brain kept replaying the events of the night, revolving in circles like the slow-moving ceiling fan above me.

It hadn't felt like a dream. The feel of his rough tongue licking the sticky marshmallow from my fingers certainly had felt all too real.

"What's worse?" I mumbled out loud. "Having a conversation with a mythical monster that protects the swamp or having your brain trick you into thinking you're having a conversation with a mythical monster that protects the swamp? A sexy-as-hell monster at that."

At the very least, I needed to get some sleep… and probably a glass of water. But the kitchen was so far away and my body was so heavy. Instead, I pulled the pillow over my face and dropped into sleep.

THREE

My boat, *Swamp Ass*, cut through the water like butter, but the sound of the outboard motor was like a bee stinging my brain through my ears, over and over. The handful of Tylenol and huge glass of water I'd downed when I'd rolled out of bed that morning had done little to dull my headache, but errands wait for no hangover.

Cypress trees with their Spanish moss trailing in the water slid by. As I came around the bend, I couldn't help but glare at the Mileys' house. The low tin roof was mostly rust and moss at this point. The front porch, such as it was, listed drunkenly to one side. It was a wonder that the crab traps, bits of machinery, and faded red Little Tykes car with a missing wheel didn't slide straight into the water.

Guilt settled into my chest. Who was I to resent these folks taking their windfall and getting the hell out? Heaving a sigh, I opened the throttle, despite the pounding in my head, and motored past.

Just past the Mileys' were several other properties McMaster had bought. The windows in the houses were dark, like they'd been abandoned and were resigned to their fate. The buzz of chainsaws and heavy machinery broke through the sound of my motor, coming from the last property, which was being torn down. An excavator took sizable chunks out of a cabin that had sat on the property for the last eighty years. Construction workers in hard hats and sweat-drenched shirts swarmed over the area as busy as any of my bees.

Next to the construction site was a strip of trees, which gave way to a lush green lawn leading down to a brand-new dock, including a dazzlingly white boathouse and a plastic water slide. At the other end of the too-green lawn loomed a three-story behemoth of a house complete with Greek columns.

Greek columns. In the goddamn *swamp*.

I shoved sour anger down as several more modern monstrosities slid past. All new construction built by McMaster Properties. Then I was back to fishing huts and small shacks owned by people who'd lived in the swamp for generations.

As I rounded a familiar bend marked by an ancient cypress tree, a large dock came into view. A pontoon boat bobbed gently with the waves. Wooden benches ran its length under a red-and-blue-striped awning, tinged green with moss and age. Miguel, co-owner of the best swamp tour in Honey Island, must have been out with a group on the other boat.

Pulling up to the space reserved for visitors, I cut the throttle and tied the boat to a mooring cleat. The jars of honey rattled in their wooden box as I pulled them from their safe storage in the bottom of my boat and set them on the weathered dock. With a grunt, I hauled myself out of the boat and picked up the box.

The building at the end of the dock was a large, rambling affair with exposed timbers and various swamp-themed decor nailed here and there: crab traps, thick rope, and carved reliefs of crabs, crawfish, and swamp birds in flight. After transferring the box to one hip, I laid a hand on the head of the large wooden statue of an alligator that guarded the end of the dock. Hundreds of tourists' hands had worn Billy Jean's head smooth as they headed out and back from their tours.

The sign above the two French doors read, "Honey Island Swamp Tours." Cool air blasted me as I pushed open the door, sending a shiver down my sweat-slicked spine. A Formica-topped counter ran along one side of the large room. Various swamp-themed souvenirs took up the rest of the space. Racks of key chains with little plastic alligators, postcards with idyllic sunsets over cattail-filled waterways, and plushies of snakes vied for space with locally sourced arts and crafts.

"Next tour's not for another two hours," came the frazzled voice from deep within the shop.

"Like I'd want a tour of my own damn swamp," I called back.

"Heather!" Patty cried, emerging from behind a display of oyster shells, the shiny insides painstakingly painted with various Louisiana landscapes. The middle-aged white woman wore a purple T-shirt emblazoned with the tour company's logo. Strong arms enveloped me into a hug that I returned one-handed, inhaling the comforting scent of sunscreen and lavender. After a skin-cancer health scare a couple of years ago, Patty had been diligent with her sunscreen and even slathered up her husband Miguel before he took tours out, much to his grumpy annoyance.

Leaning back, Patty squeezed my shoulders. "Perfect timing. I just sold the last jar this morning."

I let her take the box from my hip and followed her to my permanent display. True enough, all the jars were gone and the yellow plastic bees and the little chalkboard sign that said "Swamp Honey. Nothin' Sweeter" were the only things left.

"Any chance of some more candles?" she asked as she stacked the jars in neat little pyramids.

"Nope. Not till at least the fall. Though it's hot enough lately, I wouldn't even have to turn on the stove to melt the wax."

Patty gave me a cheeky grin. "I figured. Still couldn't hurt to ask. I used the last one from my personal stock the other day."

"I've got a couple from last year's batch kicking around somewhere. I'll bring you one or two the next time I stop by."

"You're a peach!"

"Oh, that reminds me." I grabbed a jar from the box. "Would you mind dropping this off at Auntie Geraldine on your way home?"

"No problem. Been meaning to check up on her anyway."

Auntie Geraldine was an auntie to everyone in the swamp where she'd lived all her life. She'd had a persistent summer cough that wracked the older Black woman's thin shoulders. Tea with honey seemed to be one of the few things that helped, or at least so Auntie Geraldine claimed. Woman had a sweet tooth.

"Here, let me get your cut." Patty tucked the remaining jars under the table holding my display and went around the counter, where she began rummaging and cursing under her breath at Miguel for messing up her organization.

"Aha!" Patty cried as she stood up and slapped an envelope with my name scrawled across it onto the counter. "I'm going to have to have a talk with that husband of mine. Payments do not go in the Receipts Shoebox. Has he lost his damn mind?!"

"Thanks, Patty." I slid the envelope into the back pocket of my jean shorts. No point in counting it. I trusted Patty and Miguel. They didn't cheat the locals who sold with them. Not that they'd cheat the tourists either. Miguel and Patty knew who buttered their biscuits these days.

Yelp Reviews.

My gaze caught on the display in the glass case built into the counter. Inside was a miniature swamp scene composed of plastic ferns, blue fabric scrunched up to resemble water, and a taxidermy baby alligator. Its mouth was open, revealing small, pointed teeth. The memory of teeth flashing in the moonlight and the feeling of a tongue wrapping around my finger rose in my mind.

"Everything all right?" Patty leaned over the counter, startling me.

"Yeah. No. Yeah. I'm fine," I replied in a totally casual and very natural-sounding way. Crossing my arms over my chest, I leaned a hip onto the counter. "You've lived in the swamp a long time, right?"

"Sure. Most of my life. Why?"

"What's your thoughts on the Honey Island Swamp Monster?"

Patty let out a laugh as she straightened up. "That was definitely not where I thought you were going. It's a tall tale. Like Bigfoot or Loch Ness. Good for adding spice to a tour and selling 'I Survived the Honey Island Swamp Monster' t-shirts to tourists. Why?" She narrowed her eyes at me. "You haven't been listening to Ol' Benny, have you? That booze hound tells more fish stories than he catches actual fish."

"Nah, just been on my brain. That's all." I tried to give her a reassuring smile, but by the way she stared at me, I knew she wasn't buying it. So I gave her something else. "Did you hear about the Mileys selling out? Kind of hard to blame them for taking the money and running."

The eyebrow lowered, but her mouth pulled into a frown. "Yeah, but that's not how I heard it happened."

"What do you mean?"

"They didn't have a choice. You know how Leo Miley works construction?" She continued after I nodded. "Apparently, McMaster's golfin' buddies with the guy who owns the company Leo works for. He told Leo that if he didn't take the offer, he'd get fired and blackballed for all the legit construction companies in the state."

"Shiiiiiiit," I said in an unconscious imitation of Bubs.

"With three little ones and another on the way, Leo didn't have a lot of choice. There's rumors that the Mileys aren't the only ones McMaster's played dirty to get his hands on their property. Rumors of graffiti, places getting trashed, and even arson. He's a nasty piece of work."

Anger and guilt churned in my gut. I hadn't known they were expecting again, but I wasn't close with them. There was also a petty part of myself that was pleased at being right about McMaster and the bad feeling he'd given me. I'd rather have been wrong, but I felt a little vindicated.

"Plus, it burns my britches the way he buzzes through the swamp. No regard to the 'no wake' signs. Miguel tried to call the cops on 'em, but nothing ever came of it. He's gonna hurt someone one day, drinking and racing that souped-up fishing boat of his."

Patty had her hands on her hips, winding herself up to really settle into her rant. I'd have to nip that in the bud if I wanted to get away in the next hour or two.

"Oh, he's a complete jackass. For sure. Patty, I hate to

do this, but I gotta get back and take care of the hives. But I'll stop by with a couple of candles later this week, ok?"

"Just be careful, okay? And let us know if McMaster harasses you." She came around the counter and wrapped me in another hug. "You know you can always count on us to help you bury a body in the swamp. The tour boats are perfect for that sort of thing."

I let out a grateful laugh and returned her hug. "I'll hold you to that." After giving her another squeeze, I headed for the door.

It was only as I was starting up the motor on my boat that my hungover brain lit up like a firefly's butt. Honey had been wearing jean shorts last night. They had to be Old Benny's.

"Son of a bitch," I said with a shake of my head. The booze hound had been telling the truth. He really did get pantsed by a swamp monster.

FOUR

That night I took a couple bottles of beer, my book, and a lantern and went down to the dock. After putting the lantern on the top of a post and settling into a lawn chair, I opened a beer and surveyed the swamp. Water lapped against the dock and the shore. Night birds occasionally called to each other. A cool breeze cut through the oppressive heat left over from the day. Frogs croaked, trying to get laid.

Like me.

No. Not like me. I wasn't here to sex up an ancient swamp monster. I was just looking for his help to save the swamp from a greedy capitalist asshole. That's all. Assuming said swamp monster even existed. I was pretty sure he existed.

It was still fairly early in the night, so I cracked open my paperback and tried to read about hot vampire sex, but my brain just wouldn't cooperate. While my eyes tried to read about a tattoo artist getting railed from behind by a well-endowed member of the undead, my ears were straining for any noise of an approaching swamp monster.

At every splash or odd creature sound, my head would pop up and scan the area. At one point, I even poured a bit of my lukewarm beer into the water, to no effect.

Around two in the morning, I'd read the same page at least six times and still couldn't tell you exactly what body part was being inserted where, when a drop of rain landed on my head, making me jump.

"Just great."

Fun Bee Fact: Bees know when it's going to rain and will forage more than usual the day before to prepare.

If I'd been less distracted when I'd checked on the bees earlier in the day, I might have seen the signs. More and more raindrops plopped against the wood of the dock and broke the surface of the water. As I gathered up my things, a brilliant bolt of lightning lit up the night.

One one-thousand… two one-thousand… three —BOOM.

The storm had snuck up on me, but it sure was there now. Shielding my book with my boobs as much as I could, I made a mad dash back to the house. By the time I made it to the safety of my screened-in porch, I was drenched and my poor paperback wasn't in much better shape. Curse my small boobs and their ineffective overhang.

Leaning against the doorway, I watched another bolt of lightning streak across the sky as the rain poured down. I didn't even get to the second one-thousand when the crack of the thunder rumbled across the bayou.

There's nothing like a thunderstorm in the South. The way the air almost crackles with electricity. The rumble of the thunder reverberating in your breastbone. The way the rain lashes down in sheets so thick you can barely see through it. So long as you aren't out in it, thunderstorms are a thing of power and beauty.

Turning away from the storm, I went inside to dry out my paperback as best I could.

Lightning flashed, illuminating my bedroom for a moment through the thin curtains on my window, then the dark took over once more. The only illumination was the alarm clock radio on my bedside table, with its glowing red display, 3:28 AM, like menacing eyes in the dark.

Groaning, I purposely rolled to my other side, where I couldn't see the hateful time. Not even the soothing sounds of rain beating against my roof could put me to sleep tonight. The pillow felt hot and flat against my cheek. I leveraged myself up onto my elbow and flipped it over, punching it a few times for good measure before flopping back down. The cotton pillowcase was blessedly cool against my overheated skin. How could one side get so hot and the other stay so pleasant? It was one of the small mysteries of the universe, kinda like how an honest-to-God monster had lived in the swamp for… decades?… and no one had been the wiser. Well, except for Benny.

My tired brain kept wanting to dwell on the sharp curve of Honey's smile, the way the moonlight had shone on his scales, the surprisingly soft feel of his hand wrapped around my wrist.

Nope, I wasn't thinking about that. I was only thinking about the problem of McMaster and how I could get him to leave the swamp alone. There probably wasn't anything Honey could do to help, despite seeming so fierce and determined.

The image of Honey wearing a ripped polo embroidered with the McMaster logo, picking his teeth with a golf tee, formed in my mind. I let out a snort of a laugh.

My mind drifted back to the look in Honey's eyes as he brought my marshmallow-covered hand to his mouth. Intense and hungry. It had been a long-ass time, but I didn't think any of my partners had ever looked at me with that kind of desire before. Even the memory of it made my thighs clench and my pussy ache.

"Screw it," I murmured as I rolled onto my back. My hand skated down the soft curve of my belly to the hem of my oversized sleep shirt. Hiking it up, I slipped my hand under the band of my panties. Sweet Virgin Mary, I was already so hot and wet and my finger slipped easily between my folds and deep inside me. A part of me wondered if it was a good idea to be so worked up about someone I'd only talked to for a few hours while drunk, let alone the fact that that someone was a six-foot-tall lizard-man. The rest of me didn't give two shits.

I ground the heel of my palm against my clit as I slid my finger in and out. A little whimper escaped me as I thought about how his tongue had wrapped around my finger. If he'd been that talented just licking fluff, what would it be like if he used that tongue elsewhere? Like wrapping around my nipples. Warmth built in my gut, racing up my spine. My free hand came up to rub and pinch one nipple through the thin fabric of my shirt. I increased the pressure of my palm, making the circles faster and faster, remembering the feel of his warm, wet tongue on my skin. My muscles tensed as an orgasm rolled through me and I arched off the bed. My pussy clenched on my finger, but I couldn't help but wish it was bigger, and possibly scaly.

My body relaxed back onto the bed and I dragged in a

breath. Lightning flashed as I rolled onto my side, enjoying the quiet in my head post-orgasm. My limbs felt warm and loose as I drifted off to sleep to the sound of rain hitting the roof.

~

The next day, the storm had passed and the air was hot and heavy. Let's be honest, it was always humid in the swamp, especially in the summer, but it felt like if you tried hard enough, you could get all your daily water intake through your lungs. It was the kind of humid where you stepped outside and were instantly drenched in sweat.

So it was, you know, the perfect day to be working in an unairconditioned shed. My house had a couple of aging air conditioners and ceiling fans because that was how you survived summer in the South, but the Honey Hut had neither. If I ever won the lottery, I'd upgrade the Hut, but as it stood, I made do with opening the only window and propping the door open to catch a breeze.

The front of the Hut housed my tools and supplies while I kept the back clear except for my frame spinner. When I had first started out, Cliff helped me build a homemade extractor using a (brand-new and cleaned) garbage can, wires, and spare parts from an old manual hand mixer. A few years ago, I'd upgraded to a commercial steel extractor and it was so much easier to clean and use.

I pulled a frame full of honey from the transport box I'd filled from the hives earlier that morning. Holding it over a plastic bucket, I picked up my favorite uncapping knife. It was serrated on one side and roughly the length of a bread knife. The handle was worn until it molded perfectly to my palm. There were fancy electric knives that heated up and let you slice through the wax like butter, but no electricity, and it didn't seem worth it to haul the frames up to the house when a bit of elbow grease worked just fine.

Starting at the top edge of the rectangle, I slowly sawed the knife down the length of the frame, cutting the top layer of wax and exposing the honey and comb below. Honey and wax dripped into the bottom of the bucket. I'd separate them out and use the wax to make candles later in the year. After flipping the frame around, I uncapped the other side.

The frame went into the last open slot in the spinner. This particular model held four frames. With the lid secured, I grabbed the handle and started slowly turning it. You don't want to turn it too fast, or you'll damage the comb structure. The more of the beeswax cells you can preserve, the less work the bees will have to do to refill the honeycomb.

Fun Bee Fact: To create a pound of beeswax, bees have to eat 17–20 pounds of honey.

My thoughts went around and around like the extractor's frames. Only instead of spinning out honey, I was wondering if my conversation with a swamp monster had actually happened. If he was just a drunken hallucination, what did that say about me and my late-night fantasies?

Before I could open the extractor's spout and drain the dark golden honey through a strainer and into another bucket, there came a knock from the front of the Hut. I looked up to see Cliff pop his head into the Hut.

"Heya, Cliff." I slowed my spinning to a stop at the look on his face. "What's going on?"

"Haven't heard the news?" The thin older man was nearly vibrating with excitement.

"No, I've been working all morning," I said, straightening up and stretching my back. My tank top was basically plastered to my skin by that point. "Let's sit outside."

On my way out of the Hut, I grabbed my ancient thermos and a couple of plastic cups. In the shade of a nearby oak, we'd set up a little sitting area with mismatched lawn chairs and a small metal table.

As I lowered myself into a chair, I asked, "Want some lemonade?"

"Does a bear shit in the woods?"

It was one of Cliff's standard answers, but it always made me grin. I handed Cliff his cup. The lemonade was still wonderfully cold. It was tart from the lemons and sweet from the honey from my own bees. It was the perfect drink for a sweltering day.

Cliff made a sound of deep appreciation and then fixed me with a look. "You know that construction site up the way?"

A weird mixture of dread and anticipation churned with the lemonade in my stomach. "McMaster? Yeah, of course. He didn't spontaneously combust, did he?"

"Not quite." His eyes danced with suppressed delight.

"Come on, Cliff! If you don't tell me what's goin' on, I'm gonna pull out my phone and Google it."

"Fine, fine! Seems that sometime during the storm last night, the construction site was attacked."

"Attacked?" I repeated, sure that I'd misheard him.

Slowly, Cliff bobbed his head up and down. "Attacked. Supplies ripped apart. Equipment overturned and trashed. A construction trailer torn all to hell. The whole nine yards. The news is saying it's at least a hundred thousand dollars in damage."

A little bubble of happiness rose in my chest. I might have to find some pictures online and see if I couldn't get them printed out and framed. "Do they know who did it? I'd love to buy them a beer."

"That's the thing," Cliff said as he leaned forward in his seat, resting his forearms on the rickety table. "Wasn't a *who*. It was a *what*."

My glass stopped halfway to my mouth. "What?" Apparently, I was just going to repeat everything he said.

"They found a bunch of claw marks and animal tracks in the mud. Even found an alligator tooth embedded in a tire." The surreal feeling of the other night crept over me as Cliff continued, "Damnedest thing I've ever seen. It was like the swamp itself rose up and made sure McMaster knew he wasn't welcome here."

"We all know that's a fucking lie," McMaster bellowed.

Cliff and I turned to find McMaster storming towards us and my entire body tensed, bracing for the fight I knew was coming. Mud caked his fancy cowboy boots. His polo shirt was untucked and rumpled. Eyes narrowed on me with hate and accusation, and I couldn't help but think the veins bulging in his neck and the deep red color of his face weren't good signs.

"I know you did this," he seethed.

I forced a scoff from my throat. "Really? From what I hear, your site got attacked by a bunch of alligators and wild animals. How do you suppose I managed that? I'm not the Pied Piper of Honey Island."

Anger radiated off him as he leveled a finger at me. "You did this and tried to make it look like animals to cover your tracks."

"By myself? In a thunderstorm?"

"Oh, I'm sure you had plenty of help," McMaster replied with a glare toward Cliff, who rolled his eyes at me.

"Don't you have surveillance video? Big, fancy site like that, I'm sure you sprung for cameras. Can't you just watch those and find out who did this?"

"Someone cut the wires."

"Cut or chewed?" Cliff asked in a helpful voice.

McMaster's enraged gaze swung back towards Cliff and my smugness gave way to anger. I didn't mind McMaster's hate; I reveled in it, really, but how dare he turn it on my friends.

"Hey," I snapped out as I stood, drawing McMaster's attention back to me. "I didn't wreck your precious construction site. And if you don't believe the evidence in front of your own eyes, well then, bless your heart, I just can't help you. Now, get the hell off my property."

"This isn't over," McMaster spat toward me.

"Don't make me get my attack bees."

Fun Bee Fact: Queen bees are the only bees with smooth stingers. This means they can sting multiple times without injuring themselves.

With a final glare at both me and Cliff, McMaster finally turned and stomped his way back toward the road where I'm sure his lifted F-150 waited. Probably didn't want to mess up his chrome rims coming down my rutted, muddy drive.

When we could no longer hear his angry crashing through the woods, Cliff looked at me and one eyebrow rose. "Attack bees?"

"It's a long story." I let out a laughing breath, my shoulders finally relaxing. Looking down at my cup, I found an intrepid bee crawling around the lip. "That's my drink," I said with a gentle shoo. "Get your own." With an adorable little butt wiggle, the bee flew off.

Fun Bee Fact: Bees communicate through pheromones and smells, but also by wiggling and dancing.

"The nerve of that man. As if you had anything to do with animals tearing up his equipment." Cliff shook his head in disbelief.

"There's something I've been meaning to tell you…"

FIVE

Cliff took the existence of the Honey Island Swamp Monster better than I thought he would (or than I would have if our situations had been reversed.) But he'd "seen some shit in his sixty years on this earth. Why not an old-as-sin swamp creature?" The fact that Benny hadn't been lying about how he kept losing his pants particularly tickled Cliff.

Before he'd gone back home, Cliff had speared me with that too knowing look of his and asked, "Are you gonna be seein' this swamp monster again?"

I didn't know.

But hope had me down at the dock later that night. My book had dried out during the heat of the day. The pages were warped and wavy, but still readable. Not that I thought I'd be able to concentrate any more than I had the other night. Surprisingly, I was wrong.

"Well, that's just not sanitary," I mumbled to myself, unable to tear my eyes from the page.

"What's not?"

The book flew from my hands as a little squeak

escaped me. Apparently, this was just the week for sneaking up on Heather and scaring the life out of her. Before the book could hit the water, a dark green hand snatched it in mid-air.

The Honey Island Swamp Monster stood over me, holding my battered romance novel. His powerful chest was only a couple of feet from me and I couldn't seem to pull my gaze away. The lamplight revealed that it wasn't covered in the same scales as his arms and legs, but looked smooth and almost velvety. My hands itched to run along the ridges and planes. *Rein in that libido, woman!*

"You're here." My words came out higher and breathier than I'd meant them to.

"Well?"

"Um, sorry?" I asked, suddenly confused.

A slow smile spread across his face, igniting a fire low in my belly. "What's not sanitary?"

Heat rushed into my cheeks. "Just a scene in my book."

One eyebrow ridge rose. He took a step back and started rifling through the pages. "Guess I'll have to find the answer myself."

"Fine!" I cried, crossing my arms over my chest. "The heroine is a tattoo artist and she tattoos her own thigh. The hero is a vampire and he keeps licking the blood and ink from her thigh between tattooing bouts."

Honey stood blinking at me, with the book cracked open in his claws. Tipping his head back, he let out a rumbling laugh. "You're right. That doesn't sound sanitary at all."

"Right? I mean, if he can only drink blood, you'd think the excess ink would give him indigestion at least."

"On the upside, the tattoo wouldn't hurt since his spit would act like willow bark. Dulls pain." He held the closed book out to me.

I took it but gave him a skeptical look. "How do you know that?"

There was that smile again. He sat down on the dock, his legs stretched out beside my chair. "Could be I've read stories. Could be I've known a vampire or two in my day."

My mouth dropped open. After a moment, I snapped it closed and gave myself a mental shake. I was talking to a living swamp monster. Why was I surprised that vampires might be real as well?

"Is one of those beers for me?" he asked.

"Oh! Yes. I'm afraid it's a little warm now," I said as I twisted off the top and handed the bottle over.

"Warm beer never hurt anyone." He gave me a grateful nod before tilting the bottle up and taking a long drink. There was something very appealing about the thick line of his neck as he swallowed. "Much obliged."

"You're welcome. Though, to be fair, I owe you more than a beer considering what you got up to last night." The smile slipped from my face. "In all seriousness, thank you."

"My pleasure. I can't stand leeches or bullies and this McMaster seems to be both. His type is not welcome in my swamp."

"But I am?"

Honey took another swig of his beer before giving me a smile full of teeth and hunger. "You, Heather, are very welcome in my swamp."

My pulse quickened with the heat underlying his words. It couldn't be possible that the attraction went *both* ways… could it?

"Um." I swallowed, licking my suddenly dry lips. "Would you like to come back to the house with me? I have cold beer. We could watch the Goonies?"

He finished his beer in one long drink, got gracefully to his feet, and held a clawed hand out to me. My rough, calloused hand felt darn near dainty wrapped in his as he pulled me out of the chair. Now I was mere inches from that powerful chest I had been admiring earlier. Maybe it was the beer I'd drunk, or the relief at McMaster's construction site getting trashed, but a giddy joy rose in my chest, making me bold.

I lifted my hand up and stopped just shy of actually touching his chest. My eyes went to his, asking permission to bridge the gap. His answer was to lean forward, deliberately pressing himself against my hand. Slowly, I slid my palm over the segmented planes of his chest. My breath caught at the warm, silky texture of him. The feeling was a delightful contrast to the leathery scales that covered the rest of him. I wanted to rub my cheek against it. To press myself against that muscled softness.

A low rumble started under my hand and my eyes snapped to his. Those golden eyes were narrowed, entirely focused on my face. A part of me wondered if he wanted to eat me or fuck me. The persistent ache between my thighs hoped he'd eat me, *then* fuck me.

His hand came up and brushed a stray curl of hair from my face. After circling my ear, one claw ever-so-gently traced a line along my jaw, sending an intense shiver down my spine. It would have been so easy for him to have hurt me. With just the slightest pressure, those sharp claws could have split my skin, but the care he took nearly made me dizzy. His palm cradled my cheek. Again, I was struck by how warm he was. Despite his physical similarities to an alligator, there was nothing cold-blooded about him.

His eyes locked on my lips. "May I?"

My breath hitched in my chest as I nodded. Usually, I was the one that initiated, but I could only wait to see what he'd do next. I hadn't been with anyone in ages, but there was just something about his tall presence that I found overwhelming in a new and wonderful way.

Slowly, he leaned in and pressed his lips softly against mine. It was just the barest brush of lips before he took my mouth fully. The possessive claim of the kiss and the hot sear of his lips against mine made me gasp. I pressed myself fully against the hard plane of his chest.

He took advantage of my lips, parting to snake that impressively long tongue of his into my mouth. With almost methodical thoroughness, Honey tasted my tongue and mouth and lips. Heat and desire rolled through me with every lick, every gentle nip of his so-sharp teeth that never broke the skin, every kiss that left me breathless and yet wanting more.

Large hands smoothed over my hips and cupped my ass. Honey groaned against my mouth as he gently kneaded me. One sharp claw teased under the cuff of my jean shorts, reaching up to run along the crease where my thigh met my cheek. Little needy sounds escaped me as I pressed myself harder against him, wanting both to get away from that ticklish feeling, and also wanting so much more. Flattened against his chest, I wanted my T-shirt gone. To press my aching nipples against that velvety softness.

The hard length of him that pressed into my lower belly had my breath coming hot and heavy. I knew what that bulge meant, and my curiosity about what it might look like, what it might feel like in my hand and mouth and pussy, was almost too much to bear.

I rolled my hips, rubbing myself against him, and he rewarded me with a low growl that fired my blood. I wanted this swamp monster as hungry for me as I was for him.

Breaking away from my mouth, he kissed up my jaw to

the soft spot just below my ear. That clever tongue flicked out to taste my skin.

"Cherie, how about we head up to your house?" His voice was lower, rougher than it had been before.

Considering that I was about half a minute from stripping naked and climbing him like an oak tree right there on the dock, it was a good suggestion. This late at night my stretch of swamp was usually desolate, but you never knew. "Yes. Let's go."

He stepped back and I got an unobstructed view of the tented front of his shorts. And holy moly, what a bulge it was.

Dragging my eyes upward, I realized the predatory grin was back. Seemed my swamp monster enjoyed my looking. That was fine by me. I just needed to get him behind closed doors so I could enjoy my fill without having to worry about a bunch of drunk rednecks in an airboat catching us.

Now *there* would be one for the tabloids.

I grabbed his hand and started for the shore.

"Ain't you forgetting your book?" he asked with a grin.

I didn't bother turning around or even slowing down to answer. "Nope."

"What about the beer bottles and your lantern?"

"They'll be there tomorrow."

His low laugh made my blood and steps quicken. I led him through the house, not bothering to give him any sort of tour, and straight to my bedroom. Letting go of his hand, I turned on the bedside lamp, but left the overhead light off.

One eyebrow ridge rose.

"Maybe you can see in the dark, but I can't, and I want to see you."

That earned me an approving chuckle. "Shall I show you then, cherie?"

"Yes, please." I launched myself into a sitting position on the end of the bed, not a bit ashamed of my eagerness. He seemed to be enjoying this game just as much, if not more, than I did.

One clawed hand traveled down the front of his chest, taking a slow, meandering route before getting to his waist. He unbuttoned the fly of his jean shorts and paused, his golden eyes boring into me. Only after I made an impatient noise did he slide them off his hips.

My breath caught in my throat at the sight of his, well, frankly, *monster* cock. It was the only way to phrase it. There weren't any ridges or spikes or anything. The skin looked similar to that of his chest, but softer, more delicate, and the palest of greens.

It was also huge.

I swallowed hard as my eyes traveled from his heavy balls up the rigid shaft to the wide, flared head.

A chuckle made me drag my eyes up to where an entirely too self-satisfied smirk twisted his lips. He closed the distance between us and bent down to press a kiss to my upturned mouth. His hands encircled my waist, and with one swift motion, I found myself standing before him as he sat on the bed. I wasn't a light woman, but he'd handled my weight so effortlessly it made my head spin.

Honey leaned back on his elbows, his legs spread, and his massive cock at attention. That surreal feeling hit me again. There was something perfectly right and perfectly odd about this six-foot-tall swamp monster casually lounging at the foot of my bed. The green of his skin was offset beautifully against the backdrop of my light blue comforter. The one that I pushed to the end of the bed every night because it was always too damn hot even with the ceiling fan and AC going full blast, but couldn't quite part with because my momma had always insisted on a fully made bed.

"Your turn."

"My turn?" I repeated.

"I gave you a show," Honey replied while taking his cock in one hand and stroking up slowly. "Now, it's your turn."

"Oh." I grinned and stepped back to give myself room. Grabbing the hem of my T-shirt, I pulled it over my head in one fluid motion before tossing it to the side of the room. His eyes roamed hungrily over my small breasts and pebbled nipples—bras weren't needed for support and were just another way to collect sweat in the summer. With a flash of inspiration, I turned around and looked at him over one shoulder as I undid my shorts. He sat up a little straighter and his hand moved a little faster. With my thumbs hooked in both the waistband of my shorts and my underwear, I pulled them both down one inch, then stopped. Then I pulled them down another inch, watching as Honey's eyes devoured every new slice of skin. Another couple of inches and half of my ass was on display.

"You're killin' me, cherie," Honey groaned from the bed.

I took pity on him and shoved the fabric down my legs until I was bent double.

"Stay right there."

The quiet command in his voice froze me. Before I could move, Honey was on his knees behind me. Keeping one hand on my ass, he extracted my shorts from around my ankles, then spread my thighs open into a wider stance. With no warning, he pressed his face into my pussy.

"Oh!" I cried and reached up to brace myself against

the closed bedroom door, staying bent at the waist. No way I was going to move if that's what he wanted to do.

"You taste sweeter than honeysuckle," he said, before using that long tongue of his to explore my wet folds.

Sweet Virgin Mary, I thought my imagination was good, but I was wrong. So very wrong. That flexible, talented tongue tasted every inch of me, inside and out. Pleasure zinged up my nerves like lightning.

Small, little needy noises I didn't even know I knew how to make fell from my mouth. Heat and tension built with every skillful kiss and suck and lick until my legs were vibrating. Strong hands massaged my ass. Sharp nails pricked but never broke skin. The little bright points of pain just added another dimension to my pleasure, deepening it.

When his thin lips wrapped around my clit, sucking hard, a climax rolled through me like a thunderstorm in spring. The cry he pulled from me was jagged and raw. It was as different from the orgasm I had given myself thinking about him as a Cat 5 hurricane is from a tropical storm.

When it was over, the muscles in my body relaxed and I nearly collapsed to the carpet. Honey's arms were there to catch me. One wrapped around my waist, lowering me to his kneeling lap. I leaned back against the warm wall of his chest as I took big breaths and tried to calm my racing heart.

His arm stayed around my waist, keeping me pressed to him. His other hand rubbed soothing circles on my hip and upper thigh.

When my breathing had slowed, Honey squeezed my leg and nuzzled against the side of my neck. "You don't know how long I've wanted to get my claws on that sweet ass of yours."

"Didn't realize you were an ass man," I teased. "Good thing it's my best asset."

"Oh, I think you've many wonderful assets, cherie."

The hungry note in Honey's low voice sent my pulse racing once more. His hand left my thigh to skate over my breast and run the pad of his thumb over my nipple. With care, he pinched and teased until I was squirming in his lap, arching back to press the ass he'd so admired against his hard cock. A low groan ruffled my hair as I rolled my hips again. The arm around my middle tensed in time with my movements. I wondered what I'd need to do to get Honey to shed that careful control of his. To take me with all that raw strength he possessed. To shove his—

"Shit."

Honey immediately stilled underneath me. "Is there a problem, cherie?"

"I don't have any condoms," I explained with a deliberate roll of my hips. "It's been a long time since I've needed one."

His hand moved to my other nipple. "It's been a long time for me as well. A very long time. I don't have any illnesses, and we can't reproduce, but the choice is yours. I'd be more than happy to spend the night finding every way there is to make you scream without you riding my cock."

I let out a whimper of want as my entire body ached with need. Prying his arm from my waist, I turned around and straddled him, my arms going around his neck. His hands cupped my ass, but didn't move. Golden eyes regarded me, waiting to see what I was going to do.

"Fuck me, Honey."

His hands tightened on my ass and he stood. My arms tightened around his broad neck as he carried me to the side of the bed. He set me down and crawled between my spread thighs until he was braced over me. The head of his cock pressed into my entrance.

"So very warm. So very wet," Honey murmured as he kissed up the column of my neck.

My breathing sped up as I squirmed, wanting him deeper, wanting him to fill me, but he resisted, continuing to tease me. "That's all your doing."

"I know." He thrust forward slowly, letting me get acclimated before pushing a little farther into me. "And I plan on samplin' you again once you've come on my cock."

Fuck!

The size of him stretched me, lighting up every nerve I had. He moved over and in me, again and again. His pace started slow, but gained speed as I rolled my hips to meet his thrusts. I arched up and kissed him. His tongue hungrily invaded my mouth, tasting of himself and my own salty tang. My hands roamed along Honey's broad shoulders and down the scales of his back.

A low growl rumbled out of him as his movements sped up, becoming faster and harder. The part of my brain that was still afraid of strange noises in the dark set off a warning bell. The rest of me found the sound delectable and clenched hard around him, trying to get him to make it again. I wrapped my legs around his hips, pulling him deeper into me. My feet slid along the top of his powerful tail.

Honey tensed, his body caging me as he pulsed deep within me. A low, breathless "fuck" slipped from him. The feeling and sound of making this strong monster come undone tipped me over the cliff of my own climax.

When I came back up for air, Honey was gazing down at me with a look I couldn't decipher. He raised one claw and pushed my sweaty hair back from my face. Wonder filled my belly as I realized what that look was: tenderness.

Before I could give it too much thought, he bent down and kissed my collarbone. Then my breast bone. When he kissed my stomach, I sat up on my forearms.

"Where're you going?" I asked, puzzled.

Honey paused with his mouth poised over my sex. One eyebrow ridge rose. "I told you exactly what I was gonna do. Any objections?"

It took my orgasm-addled brain a moment before it remembered. "No, please. Sample away."

Grabbing a couple of my pillows, I propped myself up. I hadn't been able to see much during the first round, but there was no way I wasn't going to watch this time. Honey smirked up at me from between my thighs.

As this big swamp monster kept his word, I couldn't help but feel like a queen bee. It was a feeling I could definitely get used to.

The ceiling fan spun above us as we lay atop my comforter. All my limbs felt as though warm honey was melting through my veins. A snuggly satisfied swamp monster lounged on his side next to me, his hand splayed over my stomach.

Fun Bee Fact: When male drone bees orgasm, their testicles explode and then they die. I was very pleased that Honey was definitely not a male drone bee.

"Why bees?" Honey asked, his voice low.

I flopped my head over to look at him. "My grandmother, actually. She always had a garden and would plant flowers just for the bees. One day, when I was maybe eight, I got stung. So many tears, as you can imagine. In between sobs, I vowed I'd tear up every flower in the garden. That way, they'd leave and wouldn't come back. Mawmaw dried my tears and then told me firmly that I would do no such thing. That it wasn't the bees' fault I was a little shit who'd invaded their space."

He let out a chuckle.

"She taught me respect for the fuzzy little pollinators. When Mawmaw passed, she left me a little money, and I'd just gotten out of a disastrous relationship. This place coming on the market seemed… I don't know. Like one last gift from her, maybe. A new start."

Honey moved his hand from my stomach and I instantly missed the comforting pressure of it. With one claw, he traced the line of my jaw. There was no heat behind the gesture, just simple comfort. "Your Mawmaw might have given you the start, but you're the one that's made this place bloom."

Warmth filled my chest. "Thank you."

Honey sat up and looked out the window. He grumbled, leaned down, and pressed a kiss to my mouth. "I need to head out, cherie. The sun'll be up soon."

A twinge of disappointment went through me, but I pushed it away. Of course he wouldn't be able to stay. He hadn't kept hidden all these years by traipsing around a bee farm in broad daylight.

I sat up and kissed his shoulder, my hand running down his side. His tail twitched. The movement caught my eye. Scooting down the bed, I started exploring the base of his tail. Feeling the muscles of it move beneath his scales.

A clawed hand wrapped around my wrist.

"Oh, I'm sorry. Should I have not touched your tail?"

Honey sat up and nuzzled the side of my neck. "No,

cherie. You are welcome to touch everywhere, but if ya keep that up, we won't be leavin' this bed anytime soon."

The proof of his words was evident in his half-hard cock resting against his thigh.

"Come on, let's get you back to the swamp." I gave him a loud smack of a kiss before crawling out of the bed and pulling on a large T-shirt, a pair of soft shorts, and some flip-flops.

After Honey put on his shorts, I walked him out onto the back lawn.

"Maybe I could cook you dinner sometime?" I asked.

Only Honey wasn't looking at me. He stood stock still on my lawn, his reptilian face tipped towards the sky and the slits of nose opening and closing as he breathed deeply.

Dread smothered the afterglow of desire. "What is it?"

After a few more huffs, his gaze snapped to mine. "Smoke. Gasoline. And burnt sugar."

The blood drained from my face. Without another word, I turned and sprinted toward the path that led to the hives. I slowed down long enough to kick off my flip-flops —they would only trip me up—before racing off as fast as I could. My heart pounded in my ears as my feet slapped against the well-worn path. Sticks and sharp rocks bit into my soles, but I didn't even notice. My entire being was focused on getting to my bees.

I stumbled as I burst from the trail and into a night-mare. Light and heat assaulted me. Flames burst from the Honey Hut's single window and leapt into the night sky. The roof was already starting to smoke and catch.

The sight of the Honey Hut in flames was bad enough, but then I saw hive No. 3. It was a ball of flame fueled by the wood of the hive, the honey and wax of the frames, and the tiny, fuzzy bodies of my bees.

"NO!" The word ripped from me as my heart shattered, the jagged pieces of it slicing through my chest.

Something in my brain snapped. Rational thought was no longer an option. All I knew was that my bees were dying.

They were dying and I needed to save them. I loved all my hives, but No. 3 was my favorite. It was my first success on the bee farm. I'd babied it through generations of queen bees. I couldn't let it burn.

Powerful arms, like bands of steel, closed around my waist, preventing me from rushing toward the flames.

No! I have to get to them.

No matter how hard I pulled or scratched or pleaded, the arms wrapped around me wouldn't let me go.

Over the crackle and pop of the fire came an inhuman wail formed of pain and desperation. Only when soft scales pressed to the side of my head, whispering soothing sounds, did I realize that the wailing was coming from me, from my throat raw with screaming.

"The rest of the hives are safe," Honey said. "The ground's too wet from the storm for the fire to spread. Ya can't save this one, but the rest will be alright. You'll be alright. I've got you."

The words finally broke through my panic. He was right. The Honey Hut and No. 3 were the only ones on fire and it didn't seem to be spreading. That should have been a comfort, but it barely registered. I'd never felt so helpless in my life.

Turning around, I pressed my tear-streaked face into Honey's chest and sobbed. The swamp monster loosened his grip now that I was no longer trying to throw myself into the inferno that had been my favorite hive. His palms smoothed up and down my spine, petting me as he continued to make little murmurs of comfort as part of my heart burned to cinders.

SIX

A mason jar half-filled with whiskey slid in front of me.

"Thanks," I managed to croak as I wrapped my soot-smeared hand around the glass but didn't actually drink.

"Sure you don't want one, Honey?" Cliff turned to where Honey hovered in the corner of Bubs and Cliff's kitchen.

"Thank you, but no."

After pouring himself and Bubs a drink, Cliff sat down next to me at the table.

I wasn't sure what had alerted them that something was wrong. Maybe it was the smoke or my wailing, but they'd shown up to find the Honey Hut on fire and me sobbing in the arms of a six-foot-tall swamp monster.

Nobody had called the fire department. This far out in the boonies, what would've been the point? Besides, a fire truck couldn't have made it through the thick trees that separated the apiary from the road.

After a couple of hours, both the hive and the Honey Hut had burned themselves to glowing embers. Cliff had found a couple of shovels, and he and Honey had heaped dirt over the ashes till they had stopped smoking. Honey had been right; the thunderstorm had kept the flames from spreading past the one hive and the Hut. I knew I should've been grateful for that fact, but all I could feel was numb.

Afterward, I'd been herded to Cliff and Bubs' kitchen table where Cliff helped me clean and bandage my feet. My mad dash through the woods had torn them to shreds, but even then, the dull throb of them was distant. They were a minor annoyance compared to the gaping, bleeding wound where my heart had been.

Bubs paced from one side of the room to the other, his face a cloud of red anger.

"Love, you're making my head hurt. Why don't you both join us, yeah?" Cliff said, looking between Bubs and Honey.

Grumbling some creative threats against McMaster, Bubs threw his bulk into a chair. Honey moved to the chair next to me with his usual grace and spun it sideways. This allowed him to face the table but still accommodated his long length of tail.

"That just won't do," Bubs fussed as he stood up, grabbed his own chair, and headed out into the backyard.

Honey and I looked at Cliff.

The older man shook his head. "Bubs's feeling helpless. This is something he can control. Let 'im do it."

Before long, Bubs returned, carrying the chair. He thrust it out toward Honey. "Here. Swap."

The middle brace of the back had been cut away, leaving just the back frame and a hole where a tail might comfortably rest.

Honey looked up and blinked at Bubs. "You didn't need to destroy your furniture on my account."

"'S just wood. Besides, no guest of mine is going to be uncomfortable at my table."

With a grateful head nod, Honey stood and took the chair from Bubs. It took a little maneuvering, but he could sit with his tail comfortably through the back of the chair. "Thank you. Your hospitality is much appreciated."

Bubs grunted his acknowledgment and took the unaltered chair back around to the other side of the table, where he sat down. Cliff pushed the glass of whiskey back into Bubs's hands before patting his husband's arm affectionately.

Honey regarded me with those golden eyes, seeing far more than he should. "I'm sorry if my actions caused the destruction of your hive. I will make this right."

"No, this isn't your fight. I've got to deal with him myself. I shouldn't have involved you in the first place." I was used to taking care of my own problems. Sure, I'd had some help from Bubs and Cliff, but the majority of the hard work had been done by me: buying the property, rebuilding the apiary, and growing my business.

If I hadn't gotten Honey involved in the first place, maybe my bees wouldn't have been murdered.

"Did you really think McMaster was gonna to take no for an answer, Heather?" Cliff's words were gentle, but firm.

"No." The word was bitter on my tongue as I slumped into my chair. "Cliff's right. It wasn't your fault, Honey, even if McMaster blamed me for wrecking his precious construction site. More likely you just sped up his timeline."

"You can't know that," Honey argued.

A ragged sigh slipped from me. "I was going to tell you the night of the thunderstorm, but then I heard about what you did, and it kind of flew outa my head. Apparently, he threatened to blackball Leo Miley from any legit construction gigs in the state if the family didn't sell. There's also some nasty rumors of destructive scare tactics. It was only a matter of time before he did something similar with me. My bees were always going to be my weak spot." I reached over and took Honey's hand. "Like I said, it's not your fault."

The hard line of his mouth softened and he gave me a grateful squeeze.

"That boy is lower than a cottonmouth's belly and twice as mean," Bubs said with a shake of his head.

I forced a weak smile to my lips. "I'm just glad it was just the Honey Hut and a single hive. It could have been worse. He could have burned everything. Or gone after you two."

"Ha! I'd like to see that yellow-bellied skunk try."

"We're not gonna give him a chance to. I'll find a way to fix this." My voice went hard as flames danced through my memories. "I will make him pay."

"*We* will make him pay," Honey corrected me. When I started shaking my head, he continued, "This man is forcing good people from their homes. Folks who've loved and cared for this swamp all their lives. He's tearing that down and bringing in people who have more money than sense. Even if I wasn't tasked with keeping the balance of the swamp, I couldn't let what he's done to you stand."

"Why? You hardly know me." The words were a near whisper. We'd known each other only a couple of days. A few kisses (ok, more than a few kisses) and some marshmallows and beers do not a lasting relationship make. Even if that traitorous, romantic part of my heart yearned for more. That wasn't how life worked.

"But I do know you, cherie. You love this swamp with your whole heart. You help your neighbors, makin' sure they have honey for their tea when they're sick. You let Fish and Game know when someone's taken more than their fair share of gators during hunting season. Sometimes ya just sit at the end of your dock, basking in the sun and takin' deep breaths of air, like you're trying to pull the whole swamp into your lungs. And you always pour a little of your drink out for the protector of the swamp."

"But… how do you know all that?"

"Because I'm the Honey Island Swamp Monster and I know everything that happens in my swamp."

That was… kind of creepy. But also weirdly comforting. It was his swamp, after all. He was certainly the oldest living resident. "Does that mean you were watching when I lost that dare to Bubs and had to go jump off the dock naked?"

"You have a spectacular ass, cherie." His mouth curled into a smile and despite myself, my heart leapt like a minnow in my chest.

Well, that certainly brought his comments from earlier into a new light. I'd thought he'd been speaking metaphorically about having wanted to get his hands on my ass forever. Had that really only been a few hours ago? It seemed like days, or months.

With his free hand, he carefully brushed a strand of hair away from where it had been plastered to my face by soot and tears. Heat flamed in my cheeks, and, well, other places.

Cliff delicately cleared his throat. "How are you planning on dealing with McMaster?"

Honey's eyes never left mine. "Folks go missing in the swamp all the time. Boating accidents. Drunken fishin' mishaps. Run-ins with dangerous animals." His smile widened, showing off sharp, wicked teeth.

Hope bloomed in my chest, burning away the despair.

There would be time to mourn hive No. 3. Time to rebuild the Honey Hut, but right now, we had work to do.

"They sure do," I said, my own wicked smile matching his. "If I called and told him I wanted to sell, I'm sure I could lure him wherever we want."

"What can we do to help?" Cliff asked.

I turned to Bubs and Cliff. "You guys don't have to do anything. You don't need to be more mixed up in all of this."

"Horseshit."

"Bubs's right. Do ya think McMaster will stop at your land? We're family and we're going to tackle this together." Cliff took one of Bubs's hands before linking his fingers with mine. "What's our motto?"

Tears slid down my cheeks, but my voice was strong as Bubs and I recited, "Us swamp gays got to stick together."

What surprised me, though, was Honey squeezing my hand and his deep rumble reciting with us. When I looked at him, he raised one massive shoulder and gave me a wry smile. I squeezed his hand back and we got down to the dirty details of our plan.

The hillock in the middle of the swamp was exactly fifteen steps across and twenty steps wide. I knew this because I'd paced in a crisscross pattern as I waited. *Swamp Ass* was tied to the roots of the one cypress tree that occupied the island. The hillock was mostly moss and waterlogged soil and pretty soon my waders were more mud than plastic.

Every few turns, I checked my watch. It had been so long since I'd worn it. The edges of the leather were cracked and flaking. I scratched at my wrist as I paced.

The buzz of an engine turned into a roar that quieted as a sleek fishing boat slowed to navigate the tree-strewn swamp. Sunlight sparkled off the blue "go faster" stripes that ran the length of the pristine white fiberglass sides. McMaster stood at the helm, wearing dark sunglasses that probably cost more than my whole boat. The smirk on his face made him look like a modern-day pirate, like he already owned the entire swamp.

McMaster pulled the boat up close to the bit of spongy land, leapt ashore, and tied off to a cypress stump. He had a black leather portfolio in his hand.

"Heather, I heard about what happened." McMaster's mouth pulled into a bad photocopy of a concerned frown. "Such a tragedy."

I'd never wanted to punch someone so badly in my life, but I didn't let my anger show. Instead, I shoved it down and kept only a mask of sorrow and worry for him to see. At least I didn't have to fake those emotions.

"Now, given the situation, most developers would take advantage of your misfortune, bank on your financial loss and desperation, and lower the price of their offer, but I'm a man with principles." His smile was all innocence and goodwill.

My desire to punch him in his lying mouth intensified.

"I'm willing to make you the same offer as last time. It's more than generous and, really, you don't want this kind of accident to happen again, do you? The loss of one hive is a tragedy, but I'm sure you could recover and rebuild your business elsewhere. Heaven forbid if something were to happen to the rest of them… that would be devastating. Wouldn't it?" He held out the portfolio.

I would've rather been given a pillowcase full of angry snakes, but I took it anyway. The leather felt smooth and expensive under my work-rough fingers. Disgust and anger bubbled in my stomach as I looked through the very official-looking documents inside. With one stroke of the shiny black pen attached to the side of the portfolio, everything I'd worked so hard for over the last ten years would be gone.

"Sounds like a pile of horseshit." I snapped the portfolio closed and tossed it to the muddy ground.

The smile dropped from his face. The cottonmouth snake had shed his corporate businessman skin. "You don't seriously believe that you're going to get a better offer, do you? Because that's not going to happen, sweetheart."

"Don't call me sweetheart," I snapped. "And I'm not lookin' for a better offer. I'm not selling my land."

McMaster went still. "Pardon?"

"I'll say it more slowly for you: I'm. Not. Selling. Ever. Not to anyone else, but most certainly not to a slimy weasel like yourself."

"I thought you'd finally come to your senses. But no, you're just a fucking swamp rat with no sense of the future." The veins in his thick neck stood out. "What was the fucking point of you dragging me out here into the middle of this fucking swamp, anyway?"

Proud of my swamp rat status, I shrugged one shoulder. "Because I wanted to give you a chance to make things right."

He let out an ugly bark of a laugh. "What the hell are you talking about?"

"I know you blackmailed Leo Miley into signing over his home. You burned down my shed and murdered my bees." I spit the words at him, heavy with the pain that still cracked me in two.

His sneer was even nastier than his laugh. "Who the fuck cares about a bunch of bees? Besides, you don't have any proof of that. Even if you did, who would you tell? The cops? I play golf with the sheriff. The DA just bought one of my homes. No one would ever take your word over mine."

I shook my head slowly at him. "To be honest, I figured that was going to be your answer, but Cliff, bless his sweet heart, wanted to give you one last chance. He always tries to see the best in folks, but there's nothing but rot and greed in you."

Letting out an annoyed sigh, McMaster reached behind his back and pulled out a Glock with a custom camo handgrip. My heart ratcheted up in my chest. This wasn't a part of the plan.

"Stay exactly where you are," McMaster barked as he pointed the gun at my chest.

Despite being a Southerner my whole life, that was actually the first time I'd had a gun pointed at me, and I had to say, not my favorite experience. My knees threatened to give out from under me as sweat rolled down my back.

"Do you really think I'm an idiot? That I would meet you in the middle of bumfuck nowhere by myself and not come armed?"

"Yeah, that one's on me." I tried to keep my voice calm as I asked, "So, what's the plan?"

"You're going to sign the papers, and then I'm gonna go have a nice steak dinner to celebrate the last piece of my golf course finally falling into place."

The water behind McMaster's shoulder rippled and my muscles relaxed a fraction. "Um. Pass."

If glares were bullets, I'd have had a hole in my chest.

"Don't you play with me, girl." The angrier he became, the thicker his accent got, losing the smooth drawl money had bought him. He threw the arm not holding the gun out to the side. "Look where we are. We're in the middle of the fucking swamp. I can do whatever I want with you and no one will ever know. I could put a bullet in you and leave ya for the gators without a second thought."

"Oh, I believe you. My answer is, Go Fuck Yourself."

The barrel of the gun swung to the ground as McMaster rolled his eyes toward the sky. "Lord, give me strength. Fine. We'll do this the hard way. Maybe if I take out one of your kneecaps, you'll change your tune."

McMaster swung the gun to point at my right knee.

Turns out that, in that moment, I learned it was my favorite knee.

"Wait!" I cried, my hands coming up in front of me.

McMaster paused, cocking his head toward me.

Dropping my hands, I said, "All right, Honey."

A slow grin split McMaster's face. "See, that's a much more respectful tone. If you're smart, we'll all come out of this ahead."

"Oh, no," I replied with a shake of my head. "I wasn't calling *you* 'honey.'"

For a single second, McMaster's face scrunched in confusion. Then claws wrapped around one of McMaster's ankles. In one swift motion, his legs were yanked out from under him. McMaster let out a high-pitched yelp that was cut off when his face smashed into the mud of the little island. As he was dragged backward toward the water, his hands scrambled ineffectively against the slick mud of the island. His eye were wide with panic in his mud-splattered face. Quick as a blink, he was gone into the murky water.

I ran to the edge of the island, and my gaze locked on to the thrashing water where I'd last seen McMaster. It was a swirling mass of bodies. Black and green flashed between glimpses of tan skin and wet red. It seemed to go on forever or maybe only half a minute. Then it was over and the waves calmed till the surface of the swamp was unbroken again. I held my breath as my eyes scanned the water, looking for any sign of McMaster: a flash of polo, a bit of expensive leather boot, something.

The water rose, and Honey's head broke the surface. Within a heartbeat, he'd climbed onto the island and reached out a hand to hover next to my cheek.

His golden eyes searched my face. "You all right, cherie?"

"Yes," I said, finally remembering to breathe. I

purposely closed the distance between us, leaning into the damp but comforting feel of his hand. "Your timing is perfect."

"I do aim to please."

"Oh, you definitely do that." I let out a little laugh. My smile faded as I looked down at McMaster's discarded gun. "What are we going to do about that?"

Honey's eyes flicked from the firearm back to me. "You're going to do what you need to do and I'm gonna make sure that gun and its owner are never found. With the help of some friends, of course."

At my confused look, Honey gestured out over the water. I took in a sharp breath at the sight of at least thirty or forty alligators forming a perimeter around the island. All of their triangular heads were pointed towards us, and their eyes seemed to be locked on Honey, waiting. I'd never seen so many gators in one place before.

I let out a soft "Ho-ly shiiiitttt."

If I'd had my phone on me, I would have taken a picture or video for Miguel. He would've wet his pants in excitement and then tried to give them all marshmallows.

"Time to get to work," Honey said with a gentle bump to my shoulder. He leaned in and pressed a quick kiss to my stunned lips. "See you soon, cherie."

Before I could reply, he bent, retrieved the dropped Glock, and walked back into the swamp. There was something weirdly sexy about watching the top of Honey's bald head cut through the water. The wall of alligators parted to let him pass before forming an honor guard behind him and heading deeper into the swamp.

Faint static crackles snapped me out of my slack-jawed drooling. I scurried over to *Swamp Ass* and dug the walkie-talkie out from its hiding space. I pushed the button, silencing the steady blips of static.

"Cliff. Bubs… It's over."

"It's damn good to hear your voice, girlie." The relief made Cliff's voice thick.

I let out a breathless laugh. "Damn good to hear yours."

"Sorry for buzzing ya, but we were getting worried. Hope we didn't interrupt."

"No. I just have some cleanup, then I'll meet back up with y'all."

"Woo-hoo!" came Bubs' muffled shout.

"Let us know when you're on the way," Cliff said clearly. "Over."

Half a smile tugged at my lips as I stowed the walkie-talkie and started pulling on leather work gloves. As Honey said, "Time to get to work."

EIGHT

It had been four days since the incident in the swamp, and I still wasn't sure what I was going to do about my burnt shed or the blackened wreck of the No. 3 hive. The fact that I hadn't seen Honey wasn't helping things.

I knew I had to clear out the charred remains and start to rebuild, but I just couldn't seem to find the energy. The rest of the hives would be fine for a few days more, so instead, I spent my days at the end of my dock, chewing through my stack of unread romances. I stayed away from the paranormals though; they hit too close to home for comfort.

Cliff and Bubs had alternated keeping me company. They knew better than to pry and would just sit with me on the dock. Their quiet friendship and support meant more to me than I had the words to express.

A part of me worried I would never see Honey again. Now that McMaster was no longer a threat to the swamp, maybe he'd gone back to being the benevolent but elusive watcher he'd been before. The thought made my heart hurt, but I didn't like dwelling on that much either.

"Well, I better get back to the house. Bubs'll be back from the market soon and he always puts the groceries away wrong," Cliff said as he stood up from his chair beside me. "If you feel like it, come on up and have dinner with us later."

He pressed a kiss to my hair and headed back up the dock. Once he hit the shore, there were only the sounds of the swamp. It was a glorious afternoon, sunny and warm, but with a cool breeze that kept it from being miserable. I went back to my latest romance.

"Girl, that stableboy's the duke. Just look at his clean ass shoes. Don't fall for his shit," I muttered to myself.

"Mind if I join ya?"

The words startled me so badly, I nearly tipped out of my chair. But at the sight of Honey poised with his forearms at the end of the dock, I leapt to my feet. He hoisted himself all the way up and I had my arms wrapped around him before he was fully standing.

The two of us wobbled dangerously and I let him go, backing up as heat flared in my cheeks. "I'm sorry. I should have asked before hugging ya like that."

He shook his head, his golden eyes never leaving my face. "To be honest, I wasn't sure what kind of reception I was gonna get, given what happened."

My mouth scrunched into a frown. "What do you mean?"

Honey gestured with one clawed hand. "You watched me drag a man into the swamp to be fed to a bunch of gators. I mighta saved the tastiest bits for myself."

The thought that Honey had eaten McMaster had crossed my mind. At first it had squicked me out, but if I didn't have a problem with the gators eating him, why would I care if Honey did?

One shoulder rose in a shrug. "Yeah, but he was an

asshole who deserved it. We gave him a chance to make things right and he didn't take it. That slimeball got what he deserved. I just hope he didn't give you or any of your friends tummy aches."

Honey blinked at me for a moment before tipping his head back and letting out that rumbling laugh of his.

I grinned, then my smile dropped. "Should you be here? In the middle of the day? What if someone sees you?"

"I'll hear 'em long before they see me, cherie." He gestured one clawed-hand to the plastic stool that Bubs had brought to the dock, just in case Honey showed up again. "May I?"

"Oh, of course."

As he got settled, I sat back down in my chair. It was nice to sit with him on the dock during the day. The sun made his dark scales shimmer in fascinating ways. Somehow, it made him even more attractive.

"Are those marshmallows?" Honey asked with a wide grin.

I grabbed the bag from where it had sat under my chair for the last four days. "Yes, but not the kind we ate. Miguel, who runs the swamp tours, gave them to me. I was hoping you'd take them to the gators who helped dispose of McMaster. You know, as a thank you."

He reached out and gently squeezed one of my hands. "That's very kind of ya. They will love the treats. But, speaking of that unpleasantness, you haven't had any trouble with the authorities, have you?"

Instead of letting go, he held on to my hand, gently running the pad of his thumb over the back. I sure wasn't going to complain.

"Yeah, they found his boat abandoned in the swamp, strewn with beer cans and fishing equipment. They came around making accusations, but I have four folks who said I was on a booze cruise with them all day. Once I showed them the time-stamped pictures, there wasn't much they could pin on me."

Bubs and Cliff had taken plenty of photos while I'd been dealing with McMaster. When I'd met back up with them, I'd been tackled by Cliff, Bubs, Miguel, and Patty.

"You had me as nervous as a long-tailed cat in a room of rocking chairs, girlie," Bubs had said as he'd given me the biggest bear hug of my life.

If the cops had noticed that our smiles in pictures from before the meeting were strained or that I wasn't in the pictures for a while, well, they hadn't said anything.

"Without a body, who's to say what happened to McMaster?" I asked with a shrug. "The swamp's a dangerous place, especially for someone with more money than sense."

"Who's to say for sure?" Honey asked with a laugh in his voice. His hand stilled its petting. "If you are up to it, I'd like to take you somewhere."

"So long as you aren't taking me into the swamp to feed me to your friends." I waggled my eyebrows to let him know I was teasing.

"I want to take you into the swamp, but I promise if anyone is gonna eat you, it'll be me."

He grinned, brought my hand up to his mouth, and pressed his lips against my knuckles. A warm shiver raced down my spine.

Once Honey had led me into a less populated area of the swamp, he climbed into *Swamp Ass* with me. Whereas most dudes would try to take over at the tiller, he never even asked, preferring to sit on the middle bench. One clawed hand trailed in the dark water while the other pointed, directing me where to go. This was a good thing, since I didn't let anyone else drive my boat—not even Cliff or Bubs.

The swamp's interior was a maze of rivers, tributaries, and small waterways that all looked the same. When Honey finally directed me to a large slice of land, I was thoroughly lost. Oh, I could find my way home if I needed to—I could just head east till I hit one of the Old Pearl Rivers—but it was kind of nice not to know exactly where I was.

Honey jumped out of the boat and pulled the bow onto the shore. As I made my way to the front of the boat, he extended a hand to help me out. Half-in, half-out of the boat, I froze.

"Are those… bees?" There was a buzzing noise I'd have known anywhere, but after the fire, I wasn't sure if I could trust my hearing not to play tricks on me.

"Come and see," Honey replied, tugging on my hand to get me moving again.

He led me past ferns and trees and into a little open space. With every step, the buzzing got louder and, sure enough, there on the lower limbs of an old oak tree was a swarm. Tears pricked my eyes as I watched the thousands of bees huddling together in clumps or flying around looking for a new place to live.

Fun Bee Fact: Swarming is how bee colonies reproduce. Half the worker bees split off with one queen while the rest stay in the hive with another.

. . .

This swarm was waiting for its scout bees to come back and give information about potential new nest sites.

"I know they won't replace the hive you lost, but we thought it might help."

"We?" I asked, my voice thick with emotion.

Honey pointed off to the side where a hive box stood. Its black and gold paint sparkled where the sun hit it. Saints' colors.

A half laugh, half sob burst from me. "Cliff painted it, didn't he? He's a diehard Saints fan."

"He did," Honey said with a smile. "He and Bubs helped me set this up for ya."

Now the waterworks were really going. I'd cried more in the last week than I had in the last decade. I used the back of my wrist to swipe the tears away, desperately searching for the tough-as-nails Heather that I'd always believed myself to be.

With great care, Honey brushed away my tears. And I realized that Honey was a massive, ancient swamp monster who could snap me in half like a twig, but he always took great pains to make sure he didn't use any of that strength against me. He was always so gentle with me, not because he coddled me, but because he cared. And damn if I didn't care right back.

As my heart ached in my chest, I tugged on one loop of his jean shorts. The hem around his muscular thighs was already starting to fray and I made a mental note to buy him a new pair the next time I went to Walmart so he wouldn't have to keep harassing Ol' Benny. That man had enough problems without a swamp monster pantsing him every six months.

Honey's golden eyes had that hungry look in them that made my pulse race and my panties damp. Even as he reached around to squeeze my ass, he asked, "Don't you want to take care of the swarm first?"

"They'll still be there afterwards. Besides, I'm pretty sure you made a promise to eat me."

His breath ghosted over my neck as he chuckled. His long tongue darted out to lick at that sensitive spot just below my ear.

"Why yes, I do believe I promised that, cherie. And I always keep my promises."

I didn't know what the future held, but in the powerful arms of Honey, deep in the swamp that claimed both our hearts, with a swarm of bees happily buzzing nearby, I knew I didn't have to face it alone.

As the saying goes, us swamp gays got to stick together.

ACKNOWLEDGMENTS

The only way to describe the creation of this novella is to say it has been a rollercoaster. While it could have been another low point in my writing career, a group of dedicated, amazing writers have helped make it something wonderful. Especially all the Monster Lovers on twitter.

A huge thank you to Chace Verity for creating such a perfect cover.

Thank you my writing group, the Space Unicorns, for all their unwavering support and encouragement. I owe a lot to Krista for always keeping my writing honest and the best it can be (even if I grumble and complain along the way). Thank you to Bunny for putting up with my muppetness and always having my back. To Josh and Krister, thank you for being some of the best cheerleaders a girl could ask for. My early readers Jessica and Henry saw value in my weird little swamp monster story and their encouragement meant so much to me.

T, my partner, has always been the anchor that keeps my feet on the ground. Your unwavering support of my writing and crazy ideas means more to me than you could know.

ABOUT THE AUTHOR

Raised in New Orleans, Victoria Weyland is a PNW transplant where she lives with her partner and their hellhound. When she's not writing and reading, she enjoys playing board games with friends and traveling. She prefers her martini's like her HEAs—filthy.

Learn about Victoria's Upcoming Works:

www.victoriaweyland.com

Or join her mailing list:

Weyland News

Follow:

Twitter: @VictoriaWeyland

IG: Victoria_R_Weyland

www.ingramcontent.com/pod-product-compliance
Lightning Source LLC
Chambersburg PA
CBHW060508300726
48975CB00008B/2700